新文京開發出版股份有限公司

新世紀・新視野・新文京一精選教科書・考試用書・專業參考書

New Wun Ching Developmental Publishing Co., Ltd.
New Age · New Choice · The Best Selected Educational Publications — NEW WCDP

Vantage Vistas

A Practical Guide to English Conversation

Gerald Wayne Mills 編著

How to use Vantage Vistas
A Practical Guide to English Conversation

Vantage Vistas: A Practical Guide to English Conversation is versatile enough to use in formal classroom settings, in informal gatherings among English students, and by individuals studying English on their own. Regardless of which means of study you use, I urge you to make use of a reliable paper or online dictionary or thesaurus. I recommend Merriam-Webster online dictionary and thesaurus because it's the American standard.

Whenever possible, use English to learn English, just as you used your native language to learn your native language when you were younger. Some of your most useful tools will be reading, a dictionary, a thesaurus, and the internet. When possible, let English speak for itself. Learning will be more enjoyable and more rewarding.

Depending on your level of English ability and your confidence, you may use any of several study strategies or a combination of strategies. *Vantage Vistas: A Practical Guide to English Conversation* features the kinds of exercises and questions that are found in the newest version of the TOEIC® test.

In this textbook, lessons and exercises are grouped by subject matter. Feel free to begin with the sections that seem easiest or most interesting to you. If you wish, feel free to skip around, selecting from here and there as you would select items from a buffet.

These lessons, as you would expect, are designed to be useful and interesting, but they are more than that. They are also designed to stimulate your imagination, opening doors to new ways of looking at your surroundings and experiences. You can make your English learning an adventure in discovery and fun.

Once you've become familiar with the questions and answers in these exercises, you may want to create your own exercises for each lesson. You can go to the internet and seek further information on the vocabulary words and on the people and things discussed in the lessons. You may plan an imaginary journey abroad and begin checking actual car rentals on the internet, or you may plan a homestay in another land.

I encourage you to use your imagination and discover your own vistas in English language learning!

Vantage Vistas ◀◀

◀◀— *A Practical Guide to English Conversation* ◀◀————

Part 01   FOOD

Lesson 01 Cooking an Omelet at Home 02

Lesson 02 Mouthwatering Ways to Describe Food 08

Lesson 03 Speaking to Your Restaurant Waitress 14

Part 02   FITNESS

Lesson 04 Louise and Allen Walk along a Riverside Park.....................24

Lesson 05 Discussing Types and Benefits of Exercise 29

Lesson 06 Experiences along a Mountain Hiking Trail 35

Part 03   OUT AND ABOUT

Lesson 07 What Kind of Movies do You Like? 42

Lesson 08 Discussing Plans for the Night Market 46

Lesson 09 Shopping in a Supermarket 52

Part 04 USEFUL "HOW-TO'S"

Lesson 10 How do I Get There from Here?.............................60

Lesson 11 How to Make a Bucket List Vacation 66

Lesson 12 How to Turn Trash into Treasure 74

Part 05 BONUS LESSON

Lesson 13 Learning to "See" the Unseen in Pictures 82

APPENDIX GLOSSARY

Vocabulary Words 90

Phrases 96

Answer 99

Part **01** Food

Lesson 01 Cooking an Omelet at Home

Lesson 02 Mouthwatering Ways to Describe Food

Lesson 03 Speaking to Your Restaurant Waitress

Lesson 01

Cooking an Omelet at Home

English Conversation

(With plenty of time before going to a movie, Daniel and Irene have decided to eat supper at Irene's apartment.)

Daniel: Irene, do you know how to cook an omelet?

Irene: Ha, ha! Just like an American. Chinese often eat supper foods for breakfast, and Americans often eat breakfast foods for supper.

Daniel: I was just asking.

(In the kitchen.)

▲ Chef's knife and cutting board

▲ Skillets on the stove

Irene: Put that cutting board and chef's knife on the counter, and put the skillet on the stove while I get the ingredients and other utensils.

(Daniel puts the cutting board and knife on the counter.)

▲ Tablespoon and tea spoon

▲ Spatulas   ▲ Grater

Irene: Let's see. Four eggs, green onions, green pepper, red pepper, ham, cheese, salt, and pepper. I'll also need a teaspoon, a spatula, an egg whisk, and a cheese grater. There. We're all set.

Daniel: I'll help if you like. Just show me how small you want me to chop the ingredients.

Irene: I'll chop the ingredients. You can whip the eggs and season them with salt and pepper. Then put a tablespoon of butter into the skillet, pour in the eggs so they cover the bottom of the pan, and heat it over a low heat.

(After chopping the green onions, green pepper, red pepper, and ham, Irene mixes the ingredients in a bowl and hands them to Daniel.)

(A few minutes later, Irene hands Daniel the chopped ingredients. Then Irene begins grating some cheese.)

Daniel: Let's see. Do I put the ingredients on just half of the egg batter?

Irene: Yes, and spread the ingredients evenly. The grated cheese goes on the other half of the batter.

(Daniel uses the spatula to spread the ingredients. Irene quickly grates some cheese into a bowl and hands it to Daniel. Daniel sprinkles the grated cheese onto the other half of the batter.)

Daniel: That melted in a hurry. Do I fold it over now?

Irene: Yes, and be careful not to tear the egg as you fold one half over the other. After you fold it over, turn off the stove and cover the skillet for three minutes.

Daniel: That was easy. I can hardly wait. It smells good.

Irene: I'll get the dishes, knives, and forks.

▲ Chef's knife, steak knife, butter knife

▲ Dishes

▲ Fork

 # Vocabulary

1-2 Listen

apartment	公寓	bowl	碗
breakfast	早餐	counter	櫃檯
cover	掩蓋	dish	盤子
ingredient	成分	ingredients	原料
mix	混合	omelet (British spelling: omelette)	煎蛋捲

recipe	食譜	space	空間
sprinkle	撒	stir	攪拌
supper	晚餐	utensil	用具
whip	打		

Utensils [用具]

chef's knife	廚師刀	cutting board	砧板
fork	叉子	grater	刨絲器
knife/knives	刀子	skillet	煎鍋
frying pan	平底鍋	spatula	抹刀
tablespoon	湯匙	whisk (whip)	打蛋器

Ingredients [原料]

black pepper	黑胡椒	butter	奶油
chopped green pepper	切碎的青椒	chopped red bell pepper	切碎的紅甜椒
chopped spring onions	切碎的蔥	egg batter	雞蛋糊
minced ham	火腿碎	salt	鹽
grated cheese	磨碎的奶酪		

1-3 Listen

💬 Phrases

all set [可以了，好了]

whip the eggs [攪拌雞蛋]

by hand [用手]

set (something) aside [把（某物）放在一邊]

spread the ingredients evenly [均勻地撒上配料]

1-4 Listen

 # Measure words

a pat of butter [一小塊奶油]

a dollop of butter [一團奶油]

tablespoon of butter [一湯匙奶油]

 # Difference between lunch, supper, and dinner

Lunch [午餐] is always the second of three meals, eaten around midday. Supper [晚餐] is always the third meal of the day, usually eaten during the early evening. Traditionally, dinner is the largest meal of the day regardless of whether it is eaten as lunch or as supper. It depends on which meal is called dinner in the culture.

 # Difference between oven and stove

An oven [烤箱] is always used for cooking food by placing the food inside the box-like appliance [器具] . The word *stove* can refer to a means of keeping a room warm, such as a wood stove [火爐] or a space heater [小型供暖器]. A kitchen stove [廚房爐灶] is usually built atop an oven, although it may be a separate appliance. A stove that's designed for cooking several things at once is called a range [爐灶]. Each cooking appliance on a range is called an eye [爐眼].

Pronunciation hint

The plural of the word dish (dishes), is pronounced with two syllables ("dish-ez"). This is also true of certain other nouns, such as bridges ("brid-jez"), kisses ("kis-sez"), witches ("wit-chez"), and mixes ("mix-ez," which may also be used as a verb). If the singular noun ends with sh, ss, ch, tch, x, or the "j" sound (as in bridge), the plural is pronounced as two syllables.

Now it's your turn!

Divide up into pairs or small groups. There are many different recipes for omelets. For example, some people like to include chopped mushrooms in their omelet recipes. Other people like to add milk to the beaten eggs and stir all the ingredients together before they cook their omelet. Some people like to heat the chopped ingredients in butter before pouring them onto the egg batter, though it requires one frying pan to heat the ingredients while using another frying pan for the egg batter. Discuss how you would create your own recipe for omelet.

You may also discuss some of your favorite recipes for other dishes and compare your recipes to your classmates' recipes for the same dishes.

Lesson

02

Mouthwatering Ways to Describe Food

2-1
Listen

 **English Conversation**

Irene: Tomorrow is the grand opening for my uncle's new restaurant. I can hardly wait.

Daniel: I wish him success.

Irene: I know what you're thinking. Restaurants are always opening and going out of business. I think my uncle knows what he's doing.

Daniel: How's that?

Irene: My uncle's restaurant not only has a variety of dishes. His dishes also have a variety of flavors and textures.

Daniel: Textures? What are food textures?

Irene: That's how the food feels in your mouth when you eat it. Like, cookies are crispy, dried mango is chewy, and mushroom soup is creamy.

Daniel: And some foods are fluffy or delicate or crunchy?

Irene: Yeah, that's it. And a juicy steak, buttered potatoes, and salmon are succulent.

Daniel: Then there are the different flavors, such as sweet, sour, and bitter.

Irene: And salty. And, although spicy hot isn't a flavor, we mustn't forget it.

Daniel: It sounds as if your uncle's restaurant has a lot of mouthwatering dishes on the menu.

Irene: His restaurant also has pleasant aromas in a relaxing atmosphere.

Daniel: It sounds great. I may go there myself.

 **Vocabulary**

aroma	香氣	bitter	苦的
bitter melon	苦瓜	coffee	咖啡
dark chocolate	黑巧克力	milk chocolate	牛奶巧克力
buttery	奶油味	salmon	鮭魚
pound cake	磅蛋糕	chewy	耐嚼的
dried mango	芒果乾	dried meat	肉乾
creamy	奶油狀的	crispy	厚實的味道
crackers	餅乾	cookie	甜餅乾
crunchy	鬆脆的	chopped nuts	切碎的堅果
delicate (flavor)	細膩的味道	A delicate food is light in flavor	溫和的味道

as well as soft	質地柔軟	and succulent (see below), rich flavor	濃郁的味道
delicious	可口的	dish (food)	菜（食物）
flavor	味道	fluffy (taste)	蓬鬆的味道
juicy	多汁的	menu	菜單
mouthwatering	垂涎三尺	palate	味覺
restaurant	餐廳	rich	濃郁
salty	鹹	sour	酸的
steak	牛排	succulent	肉質的
also	又 ... 又 ...	sweet	甜的
tart	酸	tongue	舌頭
variety	種類		

Note:

French cheese cake has a delicate texture and taste (more mouthwatering; that is, it melts in your mouth) [在你嘴裡融化]; New York cheese cake is rich and heavier.

Phrases

2-3 Listen

food texture [食物質地]

(to) go out of business [歇業]

grand opening [盛大開幕]

mushroom soup [蘑菇湯]

relaxing atmosphere [輕鬆的氛圍]

spicy hot [麻辣燙]

💬 What's the difference? Sour vs. tart.

Sour is a stronger and less pleasant taste than tart. Citrus fruits [柑橘類水果] such as pineapples [菠蘿] and oranges [橘子] are usually tart; vinegar [醋] is sour. We often think of tart tastes as being a little sweet and a little sour. For example, lemons [檸檬] are sour, but lemonade [檸檬水] is tart because it has both lemon juice [檸檬汁] and sugar [糖] in it.

Savory [美味的] vs. **delicious** [可口的]: Savory foods or drinks are pleasing to the taste without being sweet. They usually contain the food's natural oil or added salt. Examples are pizza [比薩], Chinese noodles [中式麵條], avocado [牛油果], soup [湯], tomatoes [番茄], and nuts [堅果].

Now it's your turn!

How would you describe the following foods?

▲ Pizza

▲ Baked chicken and sliced baked chicken

▲ Soft drinks, tomatoes, grapes, and crackers

▲ Pita bread with olives, vinegar sauce, and sour cream dip

▲ Small dessert cakes

▲ Bagels

How would you describe the most recent meal you've eaten? Try to use the vocabulary words.

Lesson 03

Speaking to Your Restaurant Waitress

3-1
Listen

💬 English Conversation

Waitress: Are you ready to order? *

Irene: Yes, please. I'd like fried flounder, black-eyed peas, and macaroni and cheese.** I get three vegetables?

Waitress: Yes, ma'am. That's fried flounder, black-eyed peas, and macaroni and cheese. You get one more vegetable.***

Irene: I think I'll have carrot and raisin salad.

Waitress: Would you like coffee or tea?

Irene: Ice tea****, please, with lemon, if you have it.

Waitress: Ice tea with lemon. Sweetened or unsweetened?

Irene: Sweetened, please.

Waitress: Thank you. I'll have your order shortly.

(Later)

Waitress: Are you ready to order dessert?

Irene: Yes, please. I'd like a slice of pecan pie.

Waitress: Would you like it with whipped cream?

Irene: It sounds great.

Waitress: I'll have it for you in a minute.*****

 Note:

* Or, "May I take your order?"

** Macaroni and cheese is one dish, not two. That's why we say, "macaroni and cheese is," rather than, "macaroni and cheese are." Dishes such as beans and peas are treated as plural."

*** Macaroni and cheese is not a vegetable, but some restaurants list it among the vegetables.

**** Some English speakers still spell it, "iced tea," though, with either spelling, it's pronounced, "ice tea."

***** "…in a minute…" is a figure of speech [修辭格] meaning, "soon [很快]."

Vocabulary

▲ Black-eyed peas and rice, also known as hoppin' John.

black-eyed peas	米豆	**blackberry cobbler**	黑莓餡餅
bread	麵包	**carrot and raisin salad**	胡蘿蔔葡萄乾沙拉
coffee	咖啡	**cornbread**	玉米麵包
dessert	甜點	**fried flounder**	炸比目魚
macaroni and cheese	通心粉和奶酪	**meal**	一頓飯
meat	肉	**pecan pie**	胡桃派
shortly	不久	**tea**	茶
sweetened	加糖的	**unsweetened**	不加糖的
vegetable	蔬菜	**waiter/waitress**	男／女服務生
whipping cream	淡奶油		

(Whipping cream is sometimes called whip cream, although "whip cream" is substandard English.)

 **Measure word**

3-3 Listen

sliced peaches [桃子片]

(a) slice (of) [一片]

💬 **Phrases**

3-4 Listen

Are you ready to order? [你準備好點菜了嗎？]

Will that be _____ or _____? [那會 _____ 還是不 _____ ？]

📋 **Questions**

___1. Where does this conversation take place?

    A.   In a coffee shop

    B.   At a sidewalk food stand

    C.   In a restaurant.

    D.   The dialog doesn't say.

___2. In this dialog, how many people were ordering a meal?

    A.   One

    B.   Two

    C.   More than two

    D.   The dialog doesn't say.

___3. What meat did Irene order?

    A.   Fish

    B.   Ham

    C.   Chicken

    D.   Steak

__4.   What dessert did she order?

    A.   Apple pie

    B.   Peach pie

    C.   Pecan pie

    D.   Banana puddling

__5.   Which of these did she not order?

    A.   Black-eyed peas

    B.   Carrot and raisin salad

    C.   Macaroni and cheese

    D.   Unsweetened iced tea.

7 Discussion questions

(There are no wrong answers)

1.   Why do you think she was eating alone?

2.   Which meal was she probably eating? Give reasons for your answer.

    A.   Breakfast

    B.   Lunch

    C.   Supper

    D.   A late dinner.

Now it's your turn!

    Divide up into teams of two or three. One will be the waiter or waitress. The other one or two will be customers. Place your order.

Boardwalk Restaurant Menu

3-5 Listen

Meats

fried flounder	炸比目魚	**Southern fried chicken**	南方炸雞
baked chicken	焗雞	**fried pork chop**	炸豬排
chicken fried steak	炸雞式牛排	**country fried steak**	鄉村式炸牛排
baked ham	烤火腿	**barbecued chicken**	烤雞
smoked sausage	燻香腸	**turkey and dressing**	火雞和填料

Vegetables

fried squash	炸南瓜	**macaroni and cheese**	通心粉和奶酪
black-eyed peas	米豆	**coleslow**	涼拌高麗菜
carrot and raisin salad	胡蘿蔔葡萄乾沙拉	**hoppin' john**	米豆和米飯
cabbage	高麗菜	**fresh collards**	新鮮羽衣甘藍
rice and gravy	米飯和肉汁	**green beans**	四季豆
squash casserole	砂鍋南瓜	**sliced peaches**	桃子片
potato salad	馬鈴薯沙拉	**country skillet apples**	農村煎鍋蘋果
candied yams	蜜餞山藥	**apple sauce**	蘋果醬
grilled mixed vegetables	烤混合蔬菜	**baby lima beans**	小利馬豆
jell-O	果凍	**okra and tomatoes**	秋葵和番茄

sliced tomatoes	番茄片	creamed corn	奶油玉米
mashed potatoes and gravy	馬鈴薯泥和肉汁	pickled beets	醃製甜菜
cornbread dressing with giblet gravy	玉米麵包火雞餡配內臟肉汁		

Breads 麵包

biscuits	美國烤餅	cornbread	玉米麵包

Beverages 飲料

coffee	咖啡	tea	茶

Desserts 甜點

apple pie	蘋果派	blackberry cobbler	黑莓餡餅
peach cobbler	桃子餡餅	pecan pie	胡桃派
banana pudding	香蕉布丁	carrot cake	胡蘿蔔蛋糕
chocolate cake	巧克力蛋糕	lemon meringue pie	檸檬蛋白派
vanilla ice cream	香草冰淇淋	strawberry shortcake	草莓脆餅
chocolate meringue pie	巧克力酥皮派		

Memo:

Part **02** Fitness

Lesson *04*   Louise and Allen Walk along a Riverside Park

Lesson *05*   Discussing Types and Benefits of Exercise

Lesson *06*   Experiences along a Mountain Hiking Trail

Lesson 04 — Louise and Allen Walk along a Riverside Park

 **English Conversation**

Louise: Look out, Allen. A bicycle is coming up behind us.

Allen: I see it. This walking lane along the biking path would be more convenient if it were wide enough for two people to walk side-by-side.

Louise: They probably figure that cyclists will watch where they're going.

Allen: A riverside biking path is a good place for birdwatching. I'm glad they're also watching for pedestrians.

Louise: What kind of bird is the one over there—the big black-and-white one?

Allen: Oh, that's a **Eurasian magpie**. And over there on the ground you see a flock of **Eurasian tree sparrows**.

Louise: Does that mean they're found in both Europe and Asia?

Allen: Yes, they're pretty **widespread**.

Louise: People find a lot of things to do in the riverside park: fishing, **dance practice** in an **open area beneath a bridge, working out** on **exercise equipment**, or looking at the **scenery**.

Allen: Or just walking and talking with friends.

Louise: Right now, I feel like sitting on a **bench** and **watching the world go by**.

Allen: That sounds like a winner.

Louise: Look at those birds waiting for those fishermen to throw them a fish.

Allen: The black-crowned night heron and the little egret. Each one will try to grab it before the other, but they won't fight over it. There will be enough for all of them.

 # Vocabulary

beneath	下面	bench	長椅
bridge	橋	convenient	方便的
equipment	健身器材	exercise	鍛煉
pedestrian	行人	riverside	河邊
side-by-side	並排	widespread	廣布的
bicycle	自行車	cyclist	騎自行車的人
grab	抓住	scenery	風景

Part

01

02

03

04

05

 # Names of birds in this lesson

Black-crowned night heron [黑冠夜鷺]

Eurasian magpie [歐亞喜鵲]

Eurasian tree sparrow [麻雀]

little egret [小白鷺]

 # Phrases

bicycle path/biking path [自行車道]

crown feathers [冠羽]

dance practice [實踐]

open area [開放空間]

that sounds like a winner [這聽起來是個好主意]

walking lane [步行道]

watch(ing) the world go by [看著世界過去]

working out [鍛煉]

7 Comprehension questions

___1. Which birds are mentioned in this dialog?

    A. The gray heron, the Eurasian magpie, the Eurasian tree sparrow, and the cattle egret.

    B. The black-crowned night heron, the Eurasian magpie, the Eurasian house sparrow, and the cattle egret.

    C. The black-crowned night heron, Eurasian magpie, Eurasian tree sparrow, and the little egret.

    D. The black-crowned night heron, Eurasian magpie, Eurasian tree sparrow, and the cattle egret.

__2. Which activity does this article not mention?

    A. Dance

    B. Playing games

    C. Fishing

    D. Exercise

__3. What does Allen like about the biking path?

    A. It gets him out of the house.

    B. He can use the exercise equipment.

    C. He likes to fish.

    D. It's a good place to watch birds.

__4. Who was sitting by the river?

    A. Dancers

    B. Fishermen

    C. Birds

    D. All of the above.

__5. If someone is a pedestrian, what is he not doing?

    A. Watching birds

    B. Getting exercise

    C. Dancing

    D. Enjoying the scenery.

Now it's your turn!

Do you like to go to a riverside park or bicycle path? Why or why not? What do you like to do outdoors?

Lesson 05

Discussing Types and Benefits of Exercise

English Conversation

Louise: Are you going hiking again today?

Allen: Yeah. Hiking on the nature trail is a good aerobic exercise.

Louise: I've heard that word before—aerobic and—what's the other word?

Allen: Anaerobic?

Louise: That's it—aerobic and anaerobic. What are they, and what's the difference?

Allen: Aerobic means "with oxygen" because it causes you to breathe more than usual. Aerobic exercises, such as jogging or dancing or hiking, help you to lose weight because they burn off body fat and improve your endurance.

Louise: I think that's what I need to do. What's an anaerobic exercise?

Allen: Anaerobic means "without oxygen." You don't have to breathe as much, but it takes more strength to do, and it causes your heart to beat faster. Anaerobic exercises burn off sugar, and they're good for building muscle mass.

Louise: You mean like weight lifting or pushups?

Allen: Right. And pullups—anything that requires much resistance.

Louise: When you hike uphill, doesn't that require resistance?

Allen: Any exercise calls for some resistance. If you do an aerobic exercise long enough to feel muscle pain, and you don't take a break, it becomes anaerobic. Then you're burning off sugar instead of fat.

Louise: Does that also mean you're building muscle instead of losing fat?

Allen: That's the way it works. Would you care to go hiking with me?

Louise: Only if you promise me there won't be too much resistance. I think I'm already big enough.

aerobic	有氧的	**anaerobic**	厭氧的
chin-ups	引體向上	**energy**	活力
exercise	鍛鍊	**hike/hiking**	遠足
intense	激烈的	**intensity**	強度
jog/jogging	跑步	**oxygen**	氧
pullup	引體向上	**pushup**	俯臥
stamina/ endurance	耐力	**require/requires/ calls for**	要求
resistance	阻力	**strength**	力量
uphill	上坡		

💬 Phrases

body fat [內脂肪]　　　　　　**burn off** [燃燒體]

feel pain [感到疼痛]　　　　**muscle mass** [肌肉質量]

nature trail [自然小徑]　　　**resistance training** [阻力訓練]

take a break [休息一下]　　　**weight lifting** [舉重]

💬 Difference between chin-ups and pullups

　　With chin-ups, the palms of your hands [你的手掌] are facing your shoulders [面對你的肩膀]. With pullups, the palms of your hands are facing forward [面向前方].

💬 Difference between need and require

　　Living things, such as people, animals, and plants need things. For example, we need food, water, and sunlight. Non-living things, such as cars and friendship, require things. For example, cars require gasoline, and friendships require kindness.

　　"You need to be able to sustain the activity for more than two minutes with sufficient oxygen intake,"

　　That means even as your breathing rate increases, you shouldn't find yourself gasping for air. "The intensity is usually light to moderate, so you're able to continue for about 30 to 60 minutes without spiking your heart rate significantly."

Now it's your turn!

Do you exercise to stay fit (such as aerobic or anaerobic exercises), or do you exercise for play?

If you ride a bicycle or play basketball, you're doing an aerobic exercise. If you're climbing a mountain—not just hiking—it's anerobic. Depending on how steep the trail is, it may be aerobic or anaerobic.

How many of each kind of exercise can you name?

Discuss with your teacher or classmate(s) what keeps you in shape.

Experiences along a Mountain Hiking Trail

 English Conversation

Allen: This **hiking trail** is a **relaxing** way to get some exercise.

Louise: The **boardwalk** and **safety railings** make it easier and safer to walk.

Allen: The boardwalk is kind of **steep** in some places.

Louise: Oh, I don't mind. Before the boardwalk was built, people had to walk up the steep **steps**. If older hikers can **handle** it, so can I.

Allen: In some places around here, hikers can still take the steps.

Louise: Allen, is that a cave down there next to the steps?

Allen: Yeah. It almost looks manmade, but I think it's a natural cave.

Louise: I think it is. And the cave gets enough sunlight for you to look inside.

(Later)

Allen: That waterfall is definitely manmade.

Louise: That kind of waterfall is called a cascade. The water flows over the rocks like water running down a set of steps.

Allen: This looks like a good place to rest awhile.

Louise: The pond isn't far from here. There's a bench next to the pond.

Allen: That sounds like a good rest area.

Louise: Right. We can look at the flowers, watch the ducks, and listen to the frogs.

💬 Vocabulary

6-2
Listen

bench	長椅	boardwalk	木板路
boulder	巨石	cave	洞穴
cascade	水瀑布	crag	岩
cliff	懸崖	duck	鴨子
exercise	鍛煉	flow	流動
flowers	花朵	frog	青蛙
handle	處理	listen	聽
look at / watch*	看	manmade (adjective)	人造的
natural	自然的	path	小路
pond	池塘	ramp	坡道
slope	坡	spillway	溢洪道
steps	樓梯 **	steep (adjective)	陡
waterfall	瀑布		

 Note:

*Look at/watch

Usually, you look at things that aren't moving, such as trees or flowers. You watch things that are doing something, such as ducks (swimming) or a movie. If the wind is causing trees or flowers to move, you may watch them.

**Steps/stairs

When "stairs" are found outdoors, they're usually called steps.

 **Phrases**

at the far end (of something) [在遠端] **or** [在的盡頭]

at this point [在此刻]

to catch one's breath [喘口氣]

a long drop to the bottom [長長的跌落到底部]

hiking trail [爬山徑]

next to (something) [在（某物）旁邊]

relaxing way (to) [放鬆方式]

rest area [休息區]

safety railings [安全欄杆]

stretch one's legs [散步]

📝 Comprehension Questions

(There may be more than one answer to a question, and one of the answers is misleading.)

___1. What did Louise probably mean when she said the boardwalk and safety railings made it easier and safer to walk?

    A. The boardwalk made it easier, and the safety railings made it safer.

    B. The safety railings made it easier, and the boardwalk made it safer.

    C. Neither A nor B.

    D. Both A and B.

___2. How can hikers use the trail?

    A. Use the steps.

    B. Use the boardwalk.

    C. Use neither the steps nor the boardwalk.

    D. Use both the steps and the boardwalk.

_3. What did Allen and Louise see next to the steps?

    A.   A cat

    B.   A cart

    C.   A cave

    D.   A pond.

_4. Where will Allen and Louise probably find ducks, flowers, and frogs?

    A.   The cave

    B.   The pond

    C.   The cascade

    D.   The rest area

_5. What do you think Allen and Louise will do after Allen says, "That sounds like a good rest area"?

    A.   Explore the cave.

    B.   Go home.

    C.   Stand at the rest area.

    D.   Sit on a bench.

Now it's your turn!

Do you like to go hiking? If so, where do you most like to hike? How do you prepare for the hike, and what do you do? If not, what do you like to do outdoors?

Part 03 Out and About

Lesson 07   What Kind of Movies do You Like?

Lesson 08   Discussing Plans for the Night Market

Lesson 09   Shopping in a Supermarket

Lesson 07

What Kind of Movies do You Like?

 **English Conversation**

Movies & TV [電影＆藝術]

Kevin: Selina, what kind of movies do you like?

Selina: I like just about any kind of movie as long as it's a good movie.

Kevin: People have different ideas on what a good movie would be. What kind of movie is that to you?

Selina: Oh, I don't know. I like adventure movies, comedies, and historical dramas, to name a few.

Kevin: I like all those, especially action-adventure movies. I have to admit, I also like horror movies, western movies, and martial arts movies.

Selina: Judging from your list, I'll bet you also like superhero movies.

Kevin: No, not really. Most superhero movies turn me off.

Selina: Why?

Kevin: Most superhero movies are not much more than costumes, loud noises, breaking things, and hitting each other. It's fun to watch when it's happening, but you quickly forget it, and it's just like any other superhero movie.

Selina: Yeah, I know what you mean. Most of them have so much fighting and other action that you can't really feel you get to know the characters as real people.

Kevin: And if the characters don't seem like real people to me, I don't have much reason to root for them. There's no fun in that.

Selina: And it's often hard to tell why the **heroes** and **the bad guys** are fighting each other.

Kevin: When that happens, it's hard to remember what the movie was about.

Selina: That's one thing I like about **fantasy** movies. You can feel as if you know the characters, and you can easily tell the good guys from the bad guys.

7-2
Listen

 **Vocabulary** [genre]

action	動作片	action thriller	動作驚悚片
adventure	冒險片	animation/cartoon	動畫片
biography	傳記	classics	經典片
comedy	喜劇	crime	犯罪片
documentary	記錄片	drama	戲劇
epic	史詩片	fantasy	幻想片
film noir	黑色電影	historical film	歷史片
horror	恐怖片	martial arts	武俠片
musicals/dance	音樂劇片 / 歌舞片	romance	愛情片

Part

01

02

03

04

05

romantic comedy	愛情喜劇片	science fiction	科幻片
silent movie	默片，無聲片	superhero	超級英雄片
suspense	懸念片	thriller	驚悚片
war	戰爭片	westerns	西部片

Vocabulary words [other]

| audience (n.) | 觀眾；讀者群 | (movie) character | 電影人物 |
| costume | 戲服 | hero | 英雄 |

 **Phrases**

7-3
Listen

Crime drama [罪案劇]

film, motion picture [影片，電影] [美作：(movie)]

judging from [判斷從]

movie theater [電影院]

feature-length movie, feature film [長片]

(to) root for (someone) [支持（某人）]

the bad guys [壞人]

(They) turn me off [（他們）讓我失望]

Now it's your turn!

What are your favorite movie genres? Give an example of each by giving the name of the movie. Which scene(s) did you like best, and tell why. Remember, "because it was cool" doesn't say anything about the scene; it tells only that you liked it. Instead, say something about the scene(s) that will tell us why you enjoyed it.

Lesson

08 *Discussing Plans for the Night Market*

8-1
Listen

 **English Conversation**

Selina: Kevin, do you have any plans for the weekend?

Kevin: No, nothing special. I'll probably go to the night market, but I have no other plans.

Selina: Well, the night market is special for some people. It's like social media, except in real life.

Kevin: Ha, ha! How do you mean?

Selina: When you're walking through the night market's winding alleys, you never know who you might bump into.

Kevin: Yeah, and you never know what you might find in each nook and cranny.

Selina: Oh, I love the sights, the sounds, and the aromas of the night market.

Kevin: The aromas are everywhere—ears of corn and different kinds of meat roasting over a charcoal flame or deep frying in oil.

Selina: But I don't like the odor of stinky tofu.

Kevin: I don't play any of the games they offer at the night market, but I like hearing the sounds the machines make when other people play them.

Selina: What about the sights of the night market? Food carts, low-cost knock-off merchandise, and couples walking arm in arm?

Kevin: When I went to the night market last weekend, I saw a giant, **3-D animated image** of a baby **tiger** on the side of a building. It looked real enough to touch, except that it was a **cartoon**. I stood and watched it for five minutes.

Selina: Wow! I hope it's still there. I'd like to see it myself this weekend.

Kevin: I hope so, too. It's near the north end of the night market. I'll show you.

8-2
Listen

 # Vocabulary

3-D (3-dimensional)	三維	alley	胡同
animated	動畫，類似於現場表演	aroma	香氣
cart (food cart)	餐車	cartoon	卡通片
charcoal	木炭	couple	夫妻
flame	火焰	games	遊戲

image	圖像	knock-off	仿製品
low-priced	低價	merchandise	商品
night market	夜市	odor	氣味
roast(ed/ing)	烤	sights	景點
sound	聲音	special	特別的
tiger	老虎	wind(ing) (v., adj.)	纏繞

 Phrases

8-3
Listen

arm-in-arm [手挽手]

(to) bump into (unexpectedly encounter) [不期而遇]

deep fry [油炸]

ear of corn [玉米穗]

nook and cranny [角落和縫隙]

real life [現實生活]

social media [社交媒體]

stinky tofu [臭豆腐]

Now it's your turn!

_____1. What do Kevin and Selina like about the night market?

    A.   Being surprised by what they might find.

    B.   Being surprised by whom they might meet.

    C.   The sights, sounds, and smells of the place.

    D.   All of the above.

_____2. What does Selina not like about the night market?

    A.   The knock-off merchandise.

    B.   The games at the night market.

    C.   The smell of stinky tofu.

    D.   The winding alleys.

💬 Discussion

Do you like to go to night markets? What do you like or dislike about them? Would you rather go to night markets or pedestrian [行人] daytime shopping areas? Why?

Lesson 09
Shopping in a Supermarket

 English Conversation

(Selina is in the Embonpoint Supermarket, where she bumps into Kevin.)

Selina: Oh, hi, Kevin. I'm surprised to see you here.

Kevin: My home is near here. What brings you here?

Selina: I got an advertisement in my mailbox. Embonpoint is having a sale on a new kind of shampoo—Ultra Glow they call it.

Kevin: The hair care products are on the second floor, near the escalator. I'll go with you.

Selina: You don't have to.

Kevin: It's all right. I have to buy some strawberry jam, which is also on the second floor.

(A few minutes later, as they step from the escalator...)

Selina: Oh, I see the Ultra Glow shampoo. It's on that gondola display.

Kevin: They must be having a major ad campaign for Ultra Glow. Standalone displays like that are used only for items they're really eager to promote.

Selina: Yeah. I came here especially for this. Now let's see about the jam you wanted to buy.

(A moment later…)

Kevin: That's strange. They usually have the jams here in the aisle. All I see are breakfast cereals.

Selina: I think I see it. There are several types of jam on this endcap.

Kevin: It's only a couple of steps from where they usually have it. I wonder why.

Selina: They placed it on a shelf with some kind of gourmet mustard. Anybody who is looking for jam or jelly will see the mustard. They must be promoting the mustard.

Kevin: You may be right. Endcap displays are almost as eye catching as gondola displays. While I'm here, I think I'll buy a jar of that mustard.

💬 Vocabulary

ad/advertisement	廣告	aisle	走道
retail store aisle	零售店過道	counter	櫃檯
display	展示	retail display	零售陳列
eager	渴望的	endcap	端蓋展示架
escalator	自動手扶梯	especially	尤其
gourmet	美食	jam	果醬
jar	罐	jelly	果凍
mailbox	郵箱	product	產品
promote/(sales) promotion	打折促銷	retail	零售
a sale	一筆銷售	shampoo	洗髮精
shelf	架子	(on) special/ (on) sale	特價
strawberry	草莓		

 **Phrases**

ad campaign/advertising campaign [廣告攻勢]

breakfast cereal [早餐麥片]

check-out counter [收銀台]

a couple of steps from [幾步之遙]

display island [展示島]

eye catching [引人注目]

gondola display [吊籃展示架]

hair care products [頭髮護理]

second floor [二樓]

standalone retail display [獨立零售展示]

What brings you here? [什麼風把你吹來]

Part

01

02

03

04

05

💬 Differences

Display island [展示島], endcap [端蓋展示架], gondola display [吊籃展示架], standalone retail display (a.k.a. freestanding display) [獨立零售展示].

All of them are types of standalone displays because they're not on the aisle shelves. An endcap (see photo on page 54) is found at the end of an aisle and facing away from the aisle. A display island (see photo on page 53) is completely apart from aisles, and customers can walk around it and see all sides. A gondola display is a display island that can be easily moved, sometimes allowing it to be used as an endcap.

💬 Measure words for containers

Bottle, can, cannister, carton, jar, shopping basket, shopping cart, six-pack.

💬 Some other measure words

Bunch (for grapes), gram/kilogram (weight), *jin* (Chinese unit of weight), ounce/pound (weight).

Now it's your turn!

Discuss the following with your partner(s): At which supermarket do you shop? How often do you go? What kinds of items to you buy there (for example, food items, household items, school or office supplies, clothing, electronics)? Is there something you wish your supermarket had but doesn't? If you don't shop at a supermarket, where do you prefer to buy the things I've just mentioned?

Part 04 Useful "How-to's"

Lesson 10   How do I Get There from Here?

Lesson 11   How to Make a Bucket List Vacation

Lesson 12   How to Turn Trash into Treasure

Lesson 10

How do I Get There from Here?

English Conversation

Julia: Excuse me, sir. Can you tell me how to get to the Embonpoint Supermarket?

Stranger: Oh, yes. It's not far from here. You keep going until you get to Trevor Street.

Julia: How far is Trevor Street from here?

Stranger: Trevor Street is a block from here. That's where you turn left.

Julia: Okay. I turn left on Trevor Street when I get to the traffic light?

Stranger: Right.

Julia: I thought you said left.

Stranger: I didn't mean, "Turn right." I meant you were right. Turn left.

Julia: Oh, I turn left. Then where do I go?

Stranger: Go three blocks along Trevor Street. You'll see the Cara **Department Store on the corner of Trevor Street and Travis Lane.** That's where you turn right.

Julia: Then where do I go?

Stranger: Go one block to Carmen Street. On your right, you'll see a **parking lot** on the corner of Travis Lane and Carmen Street. That's the Embonpoint Supermarket parking lot.

Julia: Is the supermarket on Carmen Street or Travis **Lane?**

Stranger: The Embonpoint supermarket is on Travis Lane, **next to** the parking lot, and **diagonally across the street from** the **community center.**

Julia: Thank you very much.

 Vocabulary

block	一個街區	boardwalk	木板路
community	社區	directions	方向
lane	巷道	right [correct]	正確的
restaurant	餐廳	right [direction]	右
stranger	陌生人	street	街道
supermarket	超級市場		

 Phrases

across from [對面]

across the street from [在 ___ 對面]

beauty shop [美容院]

between ___ and ___ [在 ___ 和 ___ 之間]

can you tell me how to___ [你能告訴我怎麼做嗎？]

department store [百貨商店]

excuse me [請問]

on your right [在你右邊]

parking lot [停車場]

swimming pool [游泳池]

traffic light [紅綠燈]

truck stop [卡車停靠站]

turn left/right [左轉／右轉]

Other useful phrases

around the corner [在角落附近]

around the corner from [從那個角落]

diagonally across the street [斜對面的街道]

next to [旁邊]

💬 Map of the Downtown Area

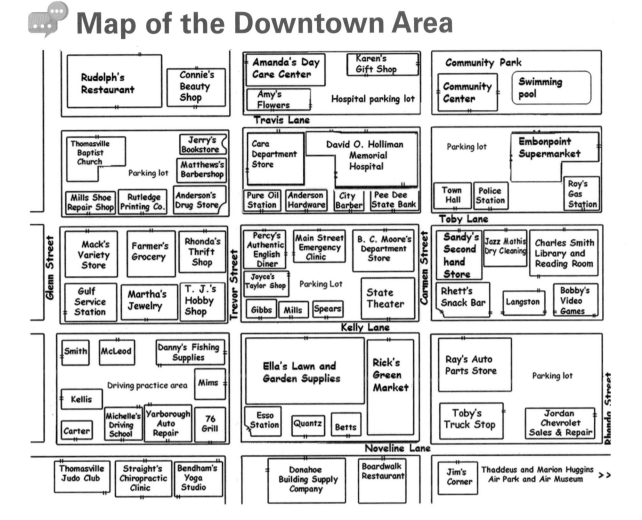

📝 Questions about Content

___1. Where is this conversation taking place?

    A.   At the corner of Carmen Street and Noveline Lane

    B.   At the corner of Kelly Street and Toby Lane

    C.   At the corner of Glenn Street and Trevor Street

    D.   At the corner of Glenn Street and Noveline Lane

__2. How many blocks does Julia have to walk to Embonpoint Supermarket?

    A.   Almost three blocks

    B.   Almost four blocks

    C.   Almost five blocks

    D.   Almost six blocks

__3. Whose home is between Rhett's Snack Bar and Bobby's Video Games?

    A.   Spears

    B.   Quantz

    C.   Langston

    D.   Smith

__4. What place is diagonally across the street from Cara Department Store?

    A.   Community Center

    B.   Connie's Beauty Shop

    C.   Amy's Flowers

    D.   David O. Holliman Memorial Hospital

__5. If you were at T. J.'s Hobby Shop on Trevor Street, what place would be around the corner from Rhonda's Thrift Shop?

    A.   Farmer's Grocery

    B.   Martha's Jewelry

    C.   Percy's Authentic English Diner

    D.   Danny's Fishing Supplies.

💬 Discussion questions

1. If you were at Connie's Beauty Shop, how would you give directions to Toby's Truck Stop?

2. If you were at Mack's Variety Store, how would you give directions to the Boardwalk restaurant?

3. Choose a partner and take turns asking directions to places on the map on the following page.

Lesson 11

How to Make a Bucket List Vacation

▲ Parasailing at Ping Lin

 # English Conversation

Julia: Patrick, do you have any plans for vacation?

Patrick: Yeah, I'm planning a bucket list vacation.

Julia: Bucket list? Do you mean like a list of things you want to do someday? It sounds strange.

Patrick: I think it makes perfect sense. I've seen a lot of bucket lists on the internet, and a vacation seems to be the best chance to do activities on your bucket list.

Julia: How do you plan a bucket list vacation?

Patrick: Well, you start by making a list of things you've always wanted to do and haven't done yet. Remember, though, it has to be something you want to do—not just going to a famous place to look at stuff.

Julia: I'd like to float on the Dead Sea without a swimming pool float. Does that count?

Patrick: Yes, but only because the Dead Sea is the only place in the world you can do that. Try to think of activities rather than places to go.

Julia: Okay, so, after you've made your bucket list, how do you turn it into a vacation?

Patrick: The list should be much longer than you'll be able to do in just one vacation. Once you've made the list, you go on the internet again and look for the best place to do five of the things on your list. You may find that the best place to do those things is not a famous place.

Julia: That's all right with me. I'll want to go on vacation to please me, not to impress other people by saying I went to a famous place.

Patrick: That's the spirit. Among other things, I'd like to go horseback riding live on a ranch, round up a herd of cattle, and go whitewater rafting.

Julia: I'd also like to ride a camel and explore a cave.

Patrick: It sounds as if we're off to a good start.

Julia: That sounds like a good idea. I may never get a chance to do all these things, but I can have fun planning a trip.

 Vocabulary

activity	活動	camel	駱駝
cattle	牛	cave	洞穴
famous	著名的	herd	放牧
impress	留下深刻印象	internet	網際網路
ranch	牧場	sightseeing	觀光
strange	奇怪的	vacation	假期

 Phrases

bucket list［遺願清單］

does that count［這算不算］

off to a good start［良好的開端］

go horseback riding［騎馬］

round up［圍捕］

swimming pool float［游泳池浮子］

that's the spirit［就是那種精神］

whitewater rafting［激浪漂流］

 Place name

Dead Sea［死海］(a place in Israel)

Now it's your turn!

Choose a partner (or partners) and make a list of at least ten things you'd like to do that you've never done before. Remember, the important word is *do*, not *see* or *go*. What do you want to do? Then decide where you can do at least five things on your bucket list. Here are some suggestions:

▲ Volunteer to help in a disaster-hit area [受災地區]

▲ Celebrate another country's holiday

▲ River tracing [河流追踪] on a white-water river [白水河] without a boat [船].

▲ Learn how to hula [草裙舞] or another traditional dance.

▲ Go parasailing [帆傘運動]

▲ Ride a horse on a beach.

▲ Explore an ancient ruin [探索古代遺跡].

▲ Wrestle a wild animal [與野生動物摔跤].

▲ Climb a mountain [爬山].

▲ Volunteer [志願者] to help people in another country.

▲ Hike [遠足] on a path [小路] that takes at least a few days to travel.

▲ Go kayaking [皮划艇].

Here are a few more suggestions

1. Jump out of an airplane (with a parachute [降落傘], of course).

2. Learn a traditional craft [傳統工藝] such as basketweaving [編籃子].

3. Participate in a safari [蘋果瀏覽器].

4. Stand in a cave with many bats [許多蝙蝠] flying all around you.

5. Scuba dive [潛水].

6. Spend some time living in a war zone [戰區].

7. Stay in an underwater hotel [水下旅館].

8. Swim with dolphins [海豚].

9. Ride in a hot air balloon [熱氣球].

10. Wrap a snake around your neck [把一條蛇繞在你的脖子上].

11. Attend a luau [烤豬宴].

12. Sleep on a boat or ship.

13. Walk on a glacier [冰川].

14. Be in a parade [遊行].

15. Walk across a rope suspension bridge [繩索吊橋]. (Seen on the following page.)

Part

01

02

03

04

05

16.   Spend a week without electronics [電子產品].

17.   Make a full-length movie [完整長度的電影] (or a short movie).

18.   Zipline [滑索].

19.   Ride an elephant [大象].

You may have already done some of the things on this list. (The author of this textbook has had twenty-two of the thirty-seven experiences mentioned in this lesson.) If you have time, tell your partner(s) about your experiences.

Lesson 12

How to Turn Trash into Treasure

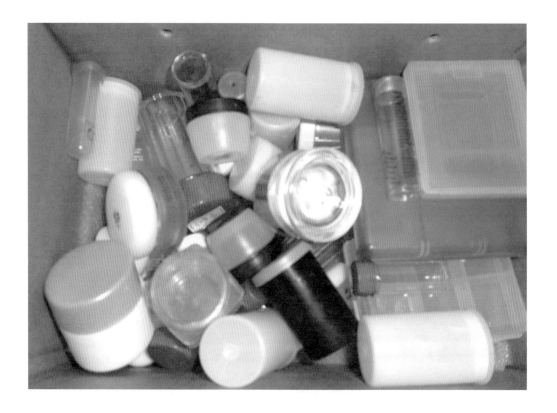

12-1 Listen

 English Conversation

Julia: I read that the three R's of caring for the environment are "reduce, recycle, and reuse." I think that's catchy.

Patrick: Don't forget "repurposing."

Julia: Repurposing? What's that?

Patrick: That means finding other uses for things after they've outlived their original purpose. For example, after you've eaten a loaf of bread, the wrapper is no longer a bread wrapper, but it's still a plastic bag.

Julia: You mean like turning trash into treasure.

 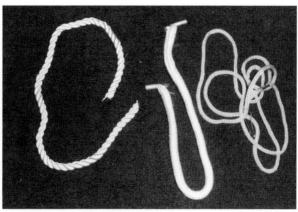

Patrick: Yeah, that's one way of looking at it. Almost two thousand years ago, Marcus Aurelius had another way of saying it. He said we should learn to see things for their basic nature and not be limited by what people believe about them.

Julia: I'm not sure what that means.

Patrick: For example, I once found a key ring on the sidewalk. I didn't need another key ring, but it was still a metal ring that could be attached to something. Two weeks later, the zipper handle on my backpack broke. The key ring turned out to be a better zipper handle than the original zipper handle.

Julia: That's nothing new. A lot of people use old things for other purposes.

Patrick: Yes, but they use them only when an idea strikes them like a bolt from the blue. If you remember what Marcus Aurelius said, you can create your own ideas instead of just letting ideas come to you. You can turn trash into treasure whenever you feel like it.

Julia: I once heard that most paper clips are used for something other than paper clips.

Patrick: Probably. A paper clip is basically a short length of wire. You can find many uses for wire.

Julia: I see. And a string handle on a paper bag is useful even after the paper bag has fallen apart.

Patrick: Yes, it's cordage, like thread or rope. Cordage is one of the most useful things you can have. Why buy it when you already have it?

 # Vocabulary

12-2
Listen

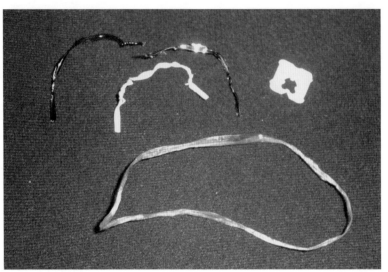

backpack	背包	**catchy**	朗朗上口
cordage	繩索	**environment**	環境
handle	把手	**(to be) limited**	（將）有限
original	原來的	**(to) outlive (something)**	（使）比（某物）長壽
purpose	目的	**recycle**	回收
reduce	減少	**repurpose**	改變用途
reuse	重用	**rope**	繩索
sidewalk	人行道	**strike**	被閃電擊中
string	細繩	**thread**	線
wire	金屬絲	**wrapper**	包裝紙

 Measure words

12-3 Listen

a bolt of lightning 一道閃電	**a length of wire** 一段電線
a loaf of bread 一塊麵包	

Phrases

12-4 Listen

(The) basic nature (of something) [（某物的）基本性質]

paper clip [回形針]

zipper handle [拉鍊把手]

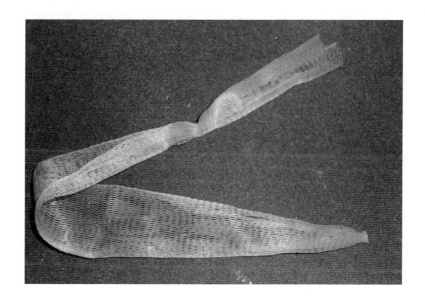

Catchy expressions

1. (To) turn trash into treasure [變廢為寶]. That means, to take an item that would be thrown out as trash, and turn it into something useful.

2. Like a bolt from the blue [就像晴朗的藍天劃過一道閃電]. That means, suddenly and unexpectedly, like a bolt of lightning on a clear day.

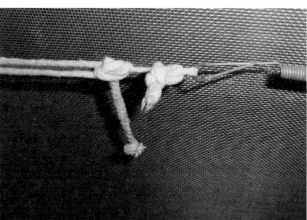

Part

01

02

03

04

05

Now it's your turn!

Your or your teacher will have to prepare for this one before class.

Collect enough recyclable items so that each member of the class will have at least one item. Make sure they're clean enough to use for this exercise.

After each member of the class has received one recyclable item, each student will be asked to tell classmates how each item can be repurposed.

To mention a few more examples of recyclable items: an empty bread wrapper, the wire that had been used to tie the bread wrapper, the plastic ring beneath the cap of a milk carton, a broken shoe lace.

In the photo above, a few disposable chopsticks were used to straighten a potted plant that had been leaning.

Use your imagination and have fun.

A Final Word on Turning Trash into Treasure

Credit card thieves no longer have to steal your credit card to get your credit information. All they have to do is brush against you in a crowded place and get a cheap credit card scanner close enough to your card to steal your information.

A Mylar® cookie wrapper may be useful in protecting your credit card information because credit card scanners are unable to scan through Mylar®. The author of this textbook has used one for years. One day, a supermarket cashier tried to scan the author's credit card before he could remove it from the Mylar® wrapper. The scanner didn't work until he removed the card from the wrapper.

Just to be on the safe side, though, you should always be careful with your credit card and other private information.

Part **05** Bonus Lesson

Lesson *13* Learning to "See" the Unseen in Pictures

Lesson

13

Learning to "See" the Unseen in Pictures

13-1 Listen

Curiosity is one of our most useful **mental assets**. It **encourages** us to look at things we can see, and use **reasoning** to **discover** things we can't see.

In lessons you've had in other classes, you've probably been asked to describe things you see in pictures. In this lesson, though, you'll be asked to tell things about the pictures that you don't really see in the pictures. You must reason from what you see.

1. Where are these young people?

2. How do they know each other?

3. What's the weather like?

4. Why are they preparing a meal outdoors?

5. What else can you tell about this picture?

1. Where is the woman in this photo?

2. What grade level students usually use this room?

3. Is this woman teaching the grade level students who usually use this room?

4. (Reasoning from 2 and 3) Is it daytime or evening?

5. What's the weather like?

6. What else can you tell about this picture?

1. Do most of the people in this picture know each other? Give reasons for your answer.

2. How did they get to this place?

3. Do they plan to go swimming?

4. What's the weather like?

5. What else can you tell about this picture?

1. These boys are looking at something. What is it?

2. Was this picture taken close to a holiday? Give reasons for your answer.

3. In what kind of place was the picture taken?

4. How tall is the building?

5. Where are the kitchen, living room, and front door?

6. How far from the television set are they sitting?

7. What else can you tell about this picture?

1. Where are these young people?

2. What kind of chess are they playing? International, Chinese, or a combination of both?

3. Of the five young people in this picture, which two are playing chess?

4. What else can you tell about this picture?

🗨️ Vocabulary

curiosity	好奇心	discover	發現
encourages	鼓勵	mental assets	精神資產
reasoning	推理		

◆ Bonus Question

What is this young woman doing? (The answer is after the Glossary.)

Memo:

Appendix

Glossary

A Practical Guide to English Conversation

Vocabulary words

A

activity	活動	ad/advertisement	廣告
aerobic	有氧的	action (as in movie)	動作片
adventure (as in movie)	冒險片	aisle	走道
retail store aisle	零售店過道	alley	胡同
anaerobic	厭氧的	animated	動畫，類似於現場表演
animation/cartoon	動畫片	apartment	公寓
aroma	香氣		

B

backpack	背包	beneath	下面
bench	長椅	bicycle	自行車
bitter	苦的	black pepper	黑胡椒
block	一個街區	bowl	碗
boardwalk	木板路	breakfast	早餐
bridge	橋	bucket list	遺願清單
butter	奶油	buttery	奶油味

C

camel	駱駝	cart (as in food cart)	餐車
cartoon	卡通片	cascade	級聯
catchy	朗朗上口	cattle	牛

cave	洞穴	(movie) character	電影人物
charcoal	木炭	chef's knife	廚師刀
chewy	耐嚼的	chin-up	引體向上
chopped	切碎的	climb	爬
comedy (as in movie)	喜劇	community	社區
convenient	方便的	cookie	甜餅乾
cordage	繩索	costume	戲服
counter	櫃檯	couple	夫妻
cover	掩蓋	cowgirl	女牛仔
creamy	奶油狀的	crispy	厚實的味道
cutting board	砧板	crunchy	鬆脆的
cyclist	騎自行車的人		

D

delicate (flavor)	細膩的味道	a delicate food is light in flavor.	溫和的味道
directions	方向	dish (food)	菜（食物）
dish (plate)	盤子	display	展示
retail display	零售陳列	drama	戲劇
duck	鴨子		

E

eager	渴望的	egg batter	雞蛋糊
endcap	端蓋展示架	endurance/ stamina	耐力
environment	環境	equipment	健身器材
escalator	自動扶梯	especially	尤其
exercise	鍛煉		

F

famous	著名的	**fantasy**	幻想片
flame	火焰	**flow**	流動
flowers	花朵	**fluffy (taste)**	蓬鬆的味道
fork	叉子	**frying pan**	平底鍋
frog	青蛙		

G

games	遊戲	**glacier**	冰川
gourmet	美食	**grab**	抓住
grater	刨絲器	**grated cheese**	磨碎的奶酪
green pepper	青椒		

H

handle (verb)	處理	**handle (noun)**	把手
herd	一群	**hero**	英雄
hike/hiking	遠足	**historical (as in movie)**	歷史片
horror (as in movie)	恐怖片		

I

image	圖像	**impress**	留下深刻印象
ingredient	成分	**ingredients**	原料
internet	網際網路		

J

jam	果醬	**jar**	罐
jelly	果凍	**jog/jogging**	跑步
juicy	多汁的		

K

knife/knives	刀子	**knock-off**	仿製品

L

lane	巷道	**(to be) limited**	（將）有限
listen	聽	**look at/watch**	看
low-priced	低價		

M

mailbox	郵箱	**manmade (adjective)**	人造的
martial arts	武俠片	**menu**	菜單
merchandise	商品	**minced ham**	火腿碎
mix	混合	**mouthwatering**	垂涎三尺
musicals/dance	音樂劇片 / 歌舞片		

N

natural 自然的	

O

odor	氣味	**omelet (British spelling: omelette)**	煎蛋捲
original	原來的	**(to) outlive [something]**	（使）比（某物）長壽
oxygen	氧		

P

pedestrian	行人	**pond**	池塘
product	產品	**promote**	推動

pullup	引體向上	purpose	目的
pushup	俯臥		

Q R

ranch	牧場	recipe	食譜
recycle	回收	red bell pepper	紅柿子椒
reduce	減少	repurpose	改變用途
require/requires/ calls for	要求	resistance	阻力
restaurant	餐廳	retail	零售
reuse	重用	right (correct)	正確的
right (direction)	右	riverside	河邊
roast(ed/ing)	烤	romance	愛情片
romantic comedy	愛情喜劇片	rope	繩索

S

(a) sale	一筆銷售	salt	鹽
salty	鹹	salmon	鮭魚
scenery	風景	science fiction	科幻片
shampoo	洗髮精	shelf	架子
shortly	不久	side-by-side	並排
sidewalk	人行道	sights	景點
sightseeing	觀光	silent movie	默片，無聲片
skillet	煎鍋	slice (a measure word)	一片
soon	很快	sound	聲音
sour	酸的	space	空間
spatula	抹刀	special	特別的
spring onions	蔥	sprinkle	撒

stir	攪拌	steak	牛排
steep (adjective)	陡	steps	樓梯
strange	奇怪的	stranger	陌生人
strawberry	草莓	street	街道
strength	力量	strike	被閃電擊中
string	細繩	succulent	肉質的
also	又 ... 又 ...	superhero	超級英雄片
supermarket	超級市場	supper	晚餐
suspense	懸念片	sweet	甜的

T

tablespoon	湯匙	thread	線
3-D (3-dimensional, three dimensional)	三維		
tiger	老虎		

U

uphill	上坡	utensil	用具

V

vacation	假期	variety	種類
vegetable	蔬菜		

W

war	戰爭片	waterfall	瀑布
westerns	西部片	whip	打
whisk (whip)	打蛋器	wind(ing) (v., adj.)	纏繞
wire	金屬絲	wrapper	包裝紙

X Y Z
(None)

Phrases

across from	[對面]
across the street from	[在 ___ 對面]
ad campaign/advertising campaign	[廣告攻勢]
arm-in-arm	[手挽手]
around the corner	[在角落附近]
around the corner from	[從那個角落]
the bad guys	[壞人]
beauty shop	[美容院]
between ___ and ___	[在 ___ 和 ___ 之間]
body fat	[內脂肪]
breakfast cereal	[早餐麥片]
[to] bump into [unexpectedly encounter]	[不期而遇]
burn off	[燃燒體]
can you tell me how to	[你能告訴我怎麼做嗎？]
a couple of steps from	[幾步之遙]
deep fry	[油炸]
department store	[百貨商店]
diagonally across the street	[斜對面的街道]
dried mango	[芒果乾]
ear of corn	[玉米穗]
excuse me	[請問]
feel pain	[感到疼痛]

eye catching	[引人注目]
food texture	[食物質地]
[to] go out of business	[歇業]
gondola display	[吊籃展示架]
grand opening	[盛大開幕]
hair care products	[頭髮護理]
hiking trail	[爬山徑]
judging from	[判斷從]
mushroom soup	[蘑菇湯]
muscle mass	[肌肉質量]
nature trail	[自然小徑]
next to [something]	[在（某物）旁邊]
night market	[夜市]
nook and cranny	[角落和縫隙]
on your right	[在你右邊]
parking lot	[停車場]
real life	[現實生活]
relaxing atmosphere	[輕鬆的氛圍]
relaxing way [to]	[放鬆方式]
rest area	[休息區]
[to] root for [someone]	[支持（某人）]
safety rails	[安全欄杆]
second floor	[二樓]
social media	[社交媒體]
spicy hot	[麻辣燙]
standalone retail display	[獨立零售展示]

stinky tofu	[臭豆腐]
swimming pool	[游泳池]
take a break	[休息一下]
traffic light	[紅綠燈]
truck stop	[卡車停靠站]
(They) turn me off	[他們] 讓我失望
turn left/right	[左轉／右轉]
variety store	[雜貨店]
weight lifting	[舉重]
what brings you here?	[什麼風把你吹來]

◆ Answer

Lesson 03: Speaking to Your Restaurant Waitress

1	2	3	4	5
C	A	A	C	D

Lesson 04: Louise and Allen Walk along a Riverside Park

1	2	3	4	5
C	B	D	B	C

Lesson 06: Experiences along a Mountain Hiking Trail

1	2	3	4	5
D	D	C	B	D

Lesson 08: Discussing Plans for the Night Market

1	2			
D	C			

Lesson 10: How do I Get There from Here?

1	2	3	4	5
D	D	C	B	A

◆ Answer to the Bonus Question in Lesson 13

That was a trick question. You probably thought she was looking at her iPhone. Actually, the picture was painted in 1860, long before cell phones were invented. What you see is a detail from ***The Expected One***, a painting by 19th century Austrian artist Ferdinand Georg Waldmüller.

She's reading her prayer book.

There are many old paintings that seem to show long-ago people using iPhones. It's unwise to judge other people's behavior by our own experiences.

Memo:

Memo:

Vantage Vistas ― A Practical Guide to
English Conversation （書號：**E461**）

編 著 者	Gerald Wayne Mills
出 版 者	新文京開發出版股份有限公司
地　　址	新北市中和區中山路二段 362 號 9 樓
電　　話	(02) 2244-8188（代表號）
F A X	(02) 2244-8189
郵　　撥	1958730-2
初　　版	西元 2024 年 01 月 10 日

有著作權　不准翻印　　　　　　　建議售價：390 元

法律顧問：蕭雄淋律師

ISBN　978-986-430-994-8

新文京開發出版股份有限公司
NEW
WCDP
新世紀‧新視野‧新文京一精選教科書‧考試用書‧專業參考書